I Love You More

Walking along a path one day,
a mother turned to her son
and asked,
"So, just how much
do you love me?"

Ready for the question,
the little boy took her hand
and began…

I love you quieter
than the quietest
caterpillar ever creeped.

I love you further than the furthest frog ever leaped.

I love you bigger
than the biggest
bubble ever blown.

I love you freer
than the freest
kite ever flown.

I love you higher than the highest swing ever swung.

I love you sweeter
than the sweetest
song ever sung.

I love you longer
than the longest
lollipop ever lasted.

I love you louder than the loudest rocket ship ever blasted.

I love you taller than the tallest giraffe ever grown.

I love you more,
so much more
than you've ever known.

Then he wrapped his
arms around her
with all the love that he had
and she felt it all surround her
when she gently whispered,
"know what son?..."

I love you more!

I LOVE YOU MORE THAN ANYTHING IN THE WHOLE WIDE WORLD.

I LOVE YOU MORE THAN ANYTHING IN THE WHOLE WIDE WORLD.

I love you more!

Then she wrapped her
arms around him
with all the love that she had
and he felt it all surround him
when he gently whispered,
"know what mommy?..."

I love you more,
so much more than
you've ever known.

I love you brighter
than the brightest
star ever shone.

I love you fuller
than the fullest
moon you ever knew.

I love you mightier
than the mightiest
wind ever blew.

I love you stronger than the strongest big river dam.

I love you deeper than the deepest fish ever swam.

I love you prettier
than the prettiest
flower ever found.

I love you longer
than the longest
path ever wound.

I love you taller than the tallest tree ever grew.

I love you higher
than the highest
bird ever flew

Walking outdoors one day
a little boy turned to his mother
and asked,
"Mommy, just how much
do you love me?"

Surprised at the question
but with no delay,
she replied with a smile…

I Love You More

A Big Thank You
to my MOM, Nana Pota, Grandma Anne and my sister Lynn
for helping to create my awesome family. And to my nieces and nephews, TYLER, Michaela,
CJ, and Myranda for adding so much to it. Good looking out Universe!
Love Always, Auntie Laura

To my mom,
Who has stood by me with enormous patience and love throughout all of my life's adventures
&
To Ferny,
who reminds me not to forget my childlike dreams…
Hey You Later!
Karen

Published by Sourcebooks Jabberwocky, an imprint of Sourcebooks, Inc.
P.O. Box 4410, Naperville, Illinois 60567-4410
(630) 961-3900
Fax: (630) 961-2168
www.jabberwockykids.com

Library of Congress Cataloging-in-Publication Data

Duksta, Laura.
  I love you more / by Laura Duksta ; illustrated by Karen Keesler.
     p. cm.
  Summary: In a book that begins at either side and ends in the middle, a little boy and his mother are taking a walk together when one asks "How much do you love me?" and the other provides a rhythmic response.
  1. Toy and movable books—Specimens. [1. Love—Fiction. 2. Mothers and sons—Fiction. 3. Toy and movable books.] I. Keesler, Karen, ill. II. Title.

PZ7.D8895Iaal 2007
[E]—dc22

Source of Production: O.G. Printing Productions, Ltd. Kowloon, Hong Kong
Date of Production: August 2012
Run Number: 18346

2007026988

Printed and bound in China.
OGP 10

I Love You More

By Laura Duksta

Illustrated by Karen Keesler

sourcebooks
jabberwocky